Aesop's Fables

Illustrated by

Martha Lightfoot

meadowside
CHILDREN'S BOOKS

The Hare
and the
Tortoise

A story about a not very
nice hare and a pretty
slow tortoise.

One day the tortoise said to the Hare,
"Let's have a race. I reckon I'd win."
"What???!" said the Hare.
"You? Win? Ha!
I could beat you without even trying."

"I don't think you will,"
said the Tortoise.

So all the animals got together
to watch the Tortoise race the Hare.

And once the race had started it seemed as if the Hare was probably right.

He raced so far ahead...

...past the woods,

...past the fields,   ...past the farm,

...that, when he looked back, he couldn't even see the Tortoise anymore.

As it was a hot day,
the Hare decided he had time for a rest
in a field under a cool shady tree.
"No need to hurry," thought the Hare,
"I'm going to win anyway."

And so the Hare closed his eyes
and started to doze. And, after
a while the doze became a sleep.
And, as the sun shone down,
the sleep got deeper and deeper.

Meanwhile the Tortoise
just kept plodding
steadily along.

Past the woods,
...past the fields,
...past the farm,

and past the Hare
who was still fast asleep
beneath the tree.

When the Hare finally
woke up, all he could see,
far away in the distance,
was the triumphant Tortoise
crossing the finishing line.
And by the time he got
there himself...

...all the other animals
were cheering the winner,
the Tortoise who never gave up!

The Fox
and the
Crow

A story about an extremely
sly, hungry fox and
a rather silly crow.

One day the crow found
the most wonderful piece of cheese.
Seizing it in her beak, she flew up
to the top of a nearby tree to enjoy her meal.

The Fox, tummy rumbling, picked himself up
and wandered over to beneath the tree.

"**Wow!**" he said.
"What a wonderful piece
of cheese! It does look like
you're enjoying that!"

He licked his lips
and stared upwards.

The Crow nodded, without dropping the cheese.

"And I bet you wouldn't want to share it with anyone," continued the wily Fox.

The crow shook her head.

"In fact," the Fox continued, cleaning between his knifelike claws, "that looks like a feast fit for a Queen.

"Except of course that **true Queens** are those whose voices sing out across the woods."

The Crow stopped eating
and looked at the Fox below.

"Indeed, a bird as wonderful as yourself,"
he went on, "must surely have the most
magnificent, glorious, sublime,
superb and delightful
voice that the woods
have ever heard."

The Crow had no other thoughts.
Of course she had the most **beautiful** voice!
This cultured Fox must **immediately**
hear how **wonderfully** she could sing.
And with that, she opened
her mouth
to sing.

And so the cheese tumbled
to the ground where the Fox gratefully
scooped it up before heading off on his way,
pausing only to turn around and say,

"Beautiful maybe,

but if you believe

all that you're told,

you'll soon

go hungry!"

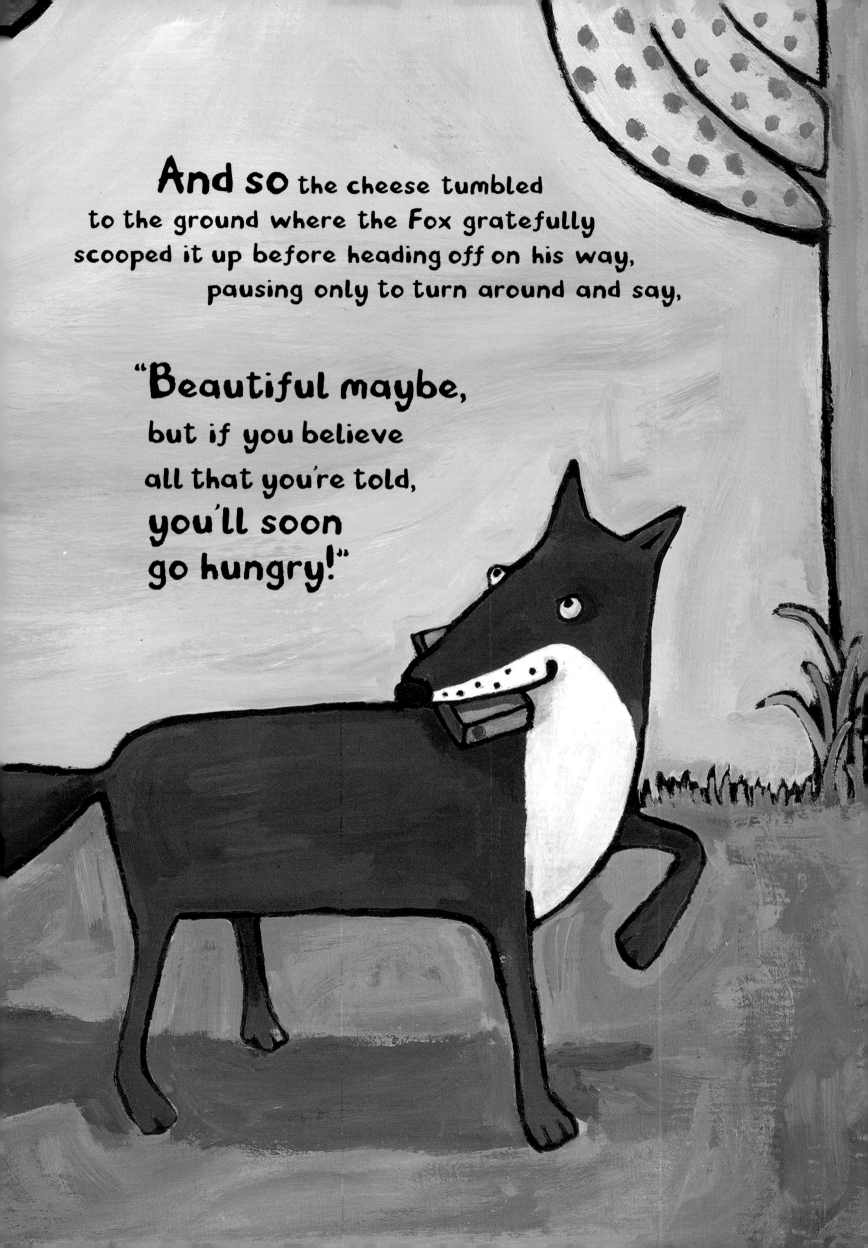

The Lion
and the
Mouse

A story about
a somewhat superior lion,
and a teeny-weeny mouse.

One day, whilst the Lion was fast asleep,
the tiny mouse was scurrying around so quickly,
that he ran straight over the Lion's head
and up his nose.

"Whoaah there, little thing!"

roared the Lion with one giant
paw holding the little Mouse,
ready to drop him into
his open mouth.

"Whoops! Oh dear sorry pardon me... oh dear, **oh dear,**" stuttered the frightened Mouse.

"Please let me go, please!

"...You never know, I might be able to help you one day."

The Lion began to laugh, and laugh **and laugh.**

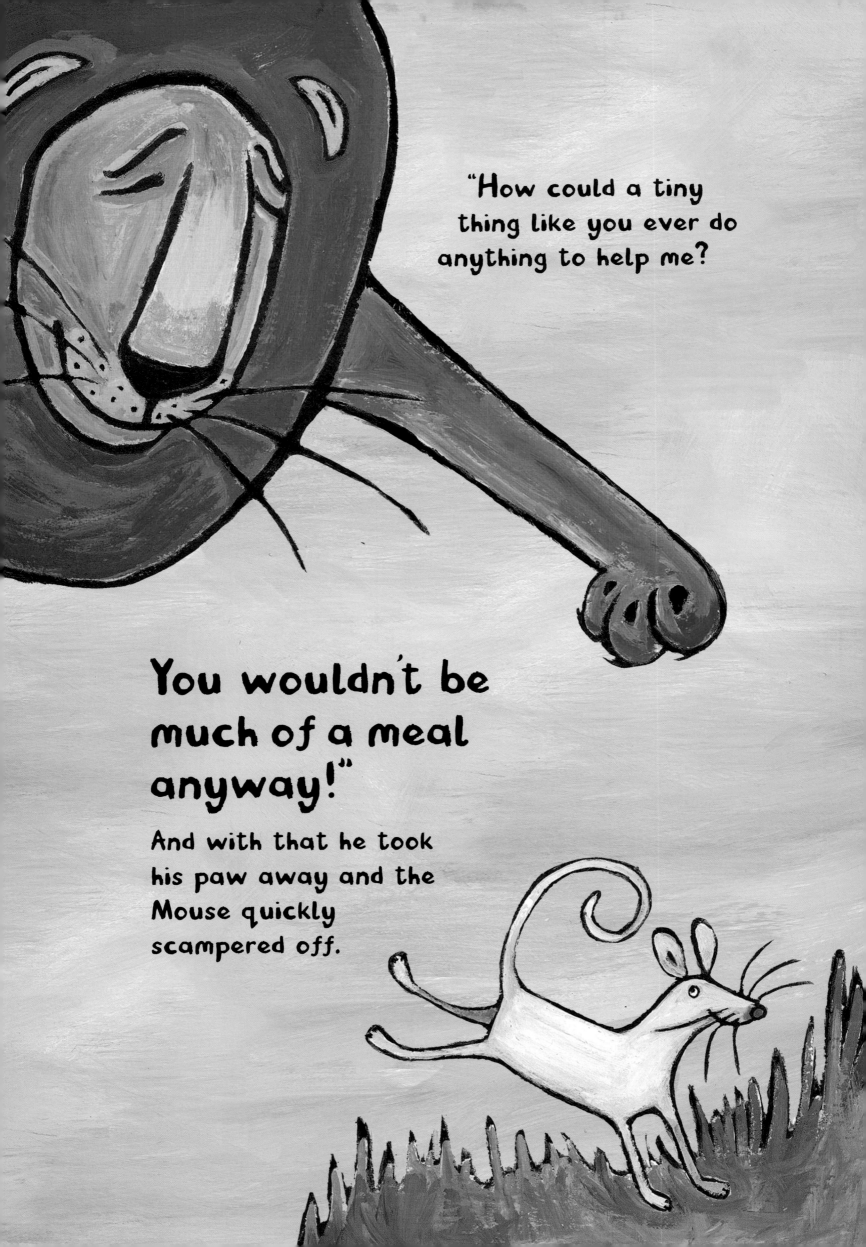

Some time after this,
in another part of the jungle,
hunters had set up a rope trap.
The Lion, who was hunting
for some food,
fell into the trap.

The tiny Mouse,
scurrying around not so far away,
heard the wounded Lion's roars.
"**Hey,** that might be the Lion
who once freed me,"
he thought.

"I wonder
if I can
help?"

And when he finally found him, he used his sharp little teeth to chew at the ropes, until they broke.

"So," said the Mouse, looking up at the huge Lion. "I saved you, didn't I?"
"Hmmm," said the Lion gently. "I may be big and you may be little.

But yes...

For **Nielsen and Conrad
and Sam Thornton**

M.L.

First published in 2006
by Meadowside Children's Books
185 Fleet Street
London EC4A 2HS

Illustrations © Martha Lightfoot
The right of Martha Lightfoot to be
identified as the illustrator has been
asserted by her in accordance with the
Copyright, Designs and Patents Act, 1988

A CIP catalogue record for this book
is available from the British Library

ISBN 10 Hbk 1-84539-220-5
ISBN 13 Hbk 978-1-84539-220-8

10 9 8 7 6 5 4 3 2 1
Printed in China